A Note to Parents and Caregivers:

Read-it! Joke Books are for children who are moving ahead on the amazing road to reading. These fun books support the acquisition and extension of reading skills as well as a love of books.

Published by the same company that produces *Read-it!* Readers, these books introduce the question/answer and dialogue patterns that help children expand their thinking about language structure and book formats.

When sharing joke books with a child, read in short stretches. Pause often to talk about the pictures and the meaning of the jokes. The question/answer and dialogue formats work well for this purpose. Have the child turn the pages and point to the pictures and familiar words. When you read the jokes, have fun creating the voices of characters or emphasizing some important words. And be sure to reread favorite jokes.

There is no right or wrong way to share books with children. Find time to read with your child, and pass on the legacy of literacy.

Adria F. Klein, Ph.D.
Professor Emeritus
California State University
San Bernardino, California

Managing Editor: Bob Temple
Creative Director: Terri Foley
Editor: Peggy Henrikson
Editorial Adviser: Andrea Cascardi
Designer: Amy Muehlenhardt
Page production: Picture Window Books
The illustrations in this book were prepared digitally.

Picture Window Books
5115 Excelsior Boulevard
Suite 232
Minneapolis, MN 55416
1-877-845-8392
www.picturewindowbooks.com

Printed in the United States of America.

Library of Congress Cataloging-in-Publication Data
Dahl, Michael.
Three-alarm jokes / written by Michael Dahl ; illustrated by Brian Jensen.
p. cm. — (Read-it! joke books)
Summary: A collection of jokes and riddles about fires and firefighters,
including, "What kind of crackers do firefighters put in their soup?
Firecrackers!"
ISBN 1-4048-0302-5
1. Fires—Juvenile humor. 2. Fire fighters—Juvenile humor. 3. Wit and
humor, Juvenile. [1. Fire fighters—Wit and humor. 2. Fires—Wit and
humor. 3. Jokes. 4. Riddles.] I. Jensen, Brian, ill. II. Title.
PN6231.F49 D34 2004
818'.5402—dc22
                                                                    2003016670

Three-Alarm Jokes

Jokes

A Book of Firefighter Jokes

Michael Dahl • Illustrated by Brian Jensen

Reading Advisers:
Adria F. Klein, Ph.D.
Professor Emeritus, California State University
San Bernardino, California

Susan Kesselring, M.A., Literacy Educator
Rosemount-Apple Valley-Eagan (Minnesota) School District

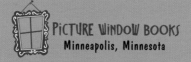

PICTURE WINDOW BOOKS
Minneapolis, Minnesota

Why do firefighters keep dogs in their stations?

To help them find the fire hydrants. 5

Why did the firefighter go to the post office?

He wanted to stamp out a fire.

What kind of crackers do firefighters put in their soup?

Firecrackers!

Man: "Drive your big red truck!"

What's the difference between a firefighter and her dog?

A firefighter wears a full suit, but the dog only pants.

Why do firefighters stay so warm at night?

They always sleep between fires.

Why did the firefighter bring his ladder to the library?

He heard the library
had a lot of stories.

Why do firefighters slide down the pole?

14 **Because they can't slide up!**

What's a firefighter's favorite dessert?

Apple crisp.

How can you tell if kids have a firefighter dad?

They're afraid to get into
water fights with him.

What kind of car does a firefighter drive?

A Blazer.

Why was the firefighter unhappy?

You're fired

Every time he worked, he got fired.

What did the boots say to the firefighter?

"You ride the truck. I'll go on foot."

How do you get down from an aerial ladder?

You don't get down from an aerial ladder.
You get down from a duck.

Why was the firefighter stressed out?

He was always alarmed.